Bible Characters Through the Ages

Book Two

Meeting Eve

Grow in faith
God Bless
Joann W Martin
12-25-16

Endorsements

Jann Martin knows how to write for kids! She combines imagination with adventure to create a chapter book that children will love. Young readers will enjoy traveling with Sarah and Daniel in their homemade time machine. In this first book of the series, readers will travel to the very beginning of time to meet Adam in the garden. Bible facts and lessons are gently woven into the story, and discussion questions at the end of the book will stimulate young minds. Once kids read this book, they well be eager for the next.

—**Crystal Bowman**, bestselling children's author

Jann Martin's most recent literary effort for children, *Bible Characters Through the Ages—Adam in the Garden,* is a compelling read for people of any age. Jann has the ability to enter into the imaginary world of a child while at the same moment appealing to those of us who are grown to allow us to return to the world we experienced growing up where "all things are possible."

From the earliest pages where the children, Daniel and Sarah, begin to imagine and to plan for "time travel," throughout their time excursion into the world of early Genesis and back home again, not wishing their parents to worry about them, the plot line pulls you eagerly forward.

While reading, I couldn't help but entertain the thought, "What if …?" Then, I suddenly realized reading Biblical traditions in a fresh and engaging way is actually like becoming a "time traveler" in a sense, where the promises of the past come alive in the present.

—Pastor Drex Morton,

St. John's Lutheran Church, Bridgewater, MI

Jann's writing will definitely keep children coming back for more. The lively language and fun element of time travel is engaging. Readers will feel a part of the story as her two main characters experience bible stories firsthand. I'm so glad this is the first in a series because readers will be waiting for the next story with great anticipation!

—Michelle Medlock Adams,

award-winning author of over forty children's books

Bible Characters Through the Ages

Book Two
Meeting Eve

Jann W. Martin

Elk Lake Publishing

Bible Characters Through the Ages Book Two:Meeting Eve

Requests for information should be addressed to:

Elk Lake Publishing, Atlanta, GA 30024

ISBN-13 Number: 978-1942513940

Graphics Design: Anna M. O'Brien

Editor: Deb Haggerty

Published in Association with Suzy Q, Inc.

Dedication

Thank you, Yahweh
for blessing me with writing for your young children.

A special thank you to my husband, Jim,
for your love, support, and being my biggest fan.

Acknowledgments

Thank you to our kids and grandkids
for your support and input.

Also to my Word Weavers friends, for your critiques,
support and suggestions.

Especially Kristen Stieffel and Kristen Hogrefe.

Bible Characters Through the Ages

Genesis 2:21-3:24

Chapter 1

"Dad's home." Mom called.

Sarah and Daniel ran to the kitchen. Daniel said, "We did it. We met Adam."

"Adam who?" Dad asked.

Daniel replied, "Adam from the Garden of Eden."

"How did you do that?"

"Mom gave Sarah and me the refrigerator box. We made a time travel machine out of the box and called it Yahweh's Express. Do you want to see?"

Dad laughed. "Of course, I'd love to see Yahweh's Express."

They all went to the playroom. Dad walked around Yahweh's Express then got down on his hands and knees and looked inside. "That's really cool. You two did a great job."

"Mom helped some." Daniel said. "But Sarah and I did most of it."

"How does it work?" Dad asked.

"Well, we sat on the pillows and Daniel said a prayer," said Sarah. "I was real scared so Daniel held my hand."

"Since I'm older, I thought I should take care of her," Daniel stood tall. "We closed our eyes and I prayed asking God to take us to meet Adam. All of a sudden, we felt like we were being lifted up and then soon gently set down. We started walking around the garden. I climbed a tree, and that's when I saw Adam.

"We walked over to him. "He was real nice. He showed us his garden, and then we went and played with the animals. After a while, Adam told us we should get back to our home but to come back to see him again.

"When we got back, no time had passed here. I don't know how that could be since we felt like we were gone for hours."

"That's quite a story." Dad smiled and winked at Mom.

"We want to go back; Eve wasn't there. I want to talk to her. Can we go back tomorrow?" asked Sarah.

Chapter 2

Dad glanced at Mom and said, "Sure, you guys can go back to the Garden of Eden. Sounds like a cool place."

"There are still a lot of animals we can see too!" Daniel added.

Mom winked at Dad. "You will have to be very careful. We don't want you two to get hurt."

"Oh, Mom," Daniel said, "you always worry about everything. Adam and Eve will be there to watch out for us. They won't let us get hurt."

"Okay," Mom said, "let's go eat our dinner before the food gets cold."

Once dinner was over, Mom said, "it's time for you two to get ready for bed. Let us know when we can tuck you in and hear your prayers."

"I'll race you," Daniel challenged Sarah.

They took off running, but Sarah beat Daniel into the bathroom. He went to his bedroom to wait his turn. Then he heard Sarah yell, "It's your turn; I'm done in the bathroom."

Once they were ready, they called for Mom and Dad to come up to Daniel's room and hear their prayers. They always said them together.

"Dear God," Daniel started, "thank you for letting us meet Adam today. We had fun seeing the garden and some of the animals. We'll go back tomorrow and meet Eve, if it's okay with you."

"Yes," Sarah said, "God, our visit was awesome. Please watch over our family as we sleep. Amen."

They didn't have school the next day, so as soon as breakfast was over, they ran to the playroom and got in Yahweh's Express. Daniel grabbed Sarah's hand and started to pray right away. They felt themselves being lifted up then gently set down.

"Make sure you leave your ballet doll, Princess, in here." Daniel said.

"Okay, if I have to,"

Chapter 3

"Come on, Sarah, let's find Adam." Daniel yelled.

"Not so fast, Daniel, I can't keep up with you!" Sarah cried.

"I'm just so excited to be back! Look, Adam is over there and Eve is with him."

They both ran together and stopped when they reached Adam and Eve.

"Hello," said Adam. "I have someone new for you to meet. While you were gone, God put me in a deep sleep. He took one of my ribs and made Eve and then he closed up my side. Now, I'm not alone. Isn't she beautiful?"

"She's very beautiful," said Sarah. "Hi, Eve. My name is Sarah and this is my brother, Daniel. It's so nice to meet you."

"It's nice to meet you, too," replied Eve. "Adam said you played with the animals yesterday. Have you been down by the water? There are some fun fish and dolphins down there."

"No." Daniel ran his fingers through his hair. "That would be fun, let's go."

"Great," replied Eve, "let's walk down to the water."

The four of them started walking. The day was sunny and quite warm.

Sarah ran ahead as soon as she saw the water and jumped in. "Come on in! The water feels great."

Daniel ran into the water. Then he disappeared. Sarah got worried. "Adam, have you seen Daniel?"

"No, I haven't. He was here just a minute ago."

Suddenly, there was a big splash. Daniel and a dolphin jumped out of the water.

"Wow, that was fun!" Daniel gasped for breath. "I went down too deep in the water. A dolphin swam over, put his nose under my feet and pushed me up real fast to the top."

Several dolphins swam around. The four of them each grabbed on to a fin and were pulled around in the water.

Then Sarah yelled, "Something hard just hit my foot!"

"Let me go look." Adam dove under the water and swam around, then came back up grinning. "It's okay, it's a sea turtle."

"Look," said Eve "There are several of them. They must have seen us in the water and came to play too."

"Can I sit on top of one?" Daniel asked.

"Sure," replied Adam. "They are very gentle and swim slow."

Sarah climbed on top of the turtle that came up next to her. She looked down into the clear water. “Look, there’s a school of fish. There are tons of them, all different kinds, shapes and colors.”

Chapter 4

"I see them," said Adam. "I had fun giving them all names." He reached down and gently picked up a silver and black fish with fins that looked like long wings. "I call this one an Angelfish." Picking up another similar fish, he added, "this is a Half-Black Angelfish; the shape is just a little different. Its wings are a little bigger, and the front is silver and the back is black. Now this one has the same shape with bigger wings and is all black. This Glasscat is long and skinny and is silver with some orange at its head."

"Look," said Sarah, "there's a fish that looks like the one I have at home."

"Yes," said Daniel, "There are so many different kinds of fish. When we get home, I want to find a book to learn more about them. I've seen them at the aquarium."

"I'm getting a little tired," said Eve. "I'm going to go back to shore."

She looked like a fish gliding through the water as she swam to shore. She sat on the beach and watched Adam and the kids play with all the fish, dolphins, and turtles. When they came to the shore, Adam said he was hungry.

"Let's go to our garden and pick some food for lunch," replied Eve. "Be careful, though. There's a serpent around here. God told us to stay away from him."

She led the way and picked some carrots, lettuce, and cucumbers. Then she found some big leaves, broke up the vegetables and placed them on the leaves and handed out their lunch.

Once everyone had their lunch, Adam folded his hands, bowed his head and began to pray. "Thank you, God, for giving us life, this beautiful place to live, new friends to talk to and especially the food Eve prepared for us. Amen."

"Thank you," said Daniel. "That was nice. What are we going to do after lunch? Can we ride the horses today? They are so beautiful and would be fun to ride."

"Sure, that's a great idea," said Adam. "Have you ever ridden a horse before?"

Chapter 5

"Yes," said Sarah, "but the horses we ride have saddles."

"What are saddles?" asked Eve.

"They're seats we strap onto the horses so we can stay on their backs," said Daniel.

"We just climb up," said Adam, "and hang onto the sides of the horse with our legs. We hold the mane in our hands."

"It's really quite easy," said Eve, "once you get used to it."

Sarah took off running. "Let's go."

She stopped near a shiny brown horse with a white stripe down its nose. "You're so pretty." Sarah patted the horse's nose and the horse whinnied and nudged her. "Does she have a name?"

"Sunshine," replied Eve. "I named her that because she is always so happy."

"How do I get on her back?" asked Sarah.

"I'll lift you up," replied Adam.

He gently picked Sarah up and set her on Sunshine's back.

"Now press your knees gently, but firmly, into her sides and grab some of her mane to keep you steady."

"But won't that hurt her?" asked Sarah, "If I pull on her hair?"

"No, not unless you pull real hard."

"Okay, I'll be careful."

Adam turned to Daniel. "Do you need help?"

"Just a little," Daniel stroked the white horse. "What is his name?"

"We call him King. He thinks he is real special. He is beautiful, but we don't want him to get too spoiled."

Then Adam climbed on an all-black horse and Eve got on her brown and white spotted horse.

"Ready?" asked Adam.

"Yep!" they said together, "let's go!"

Adam led the way and they rode through the trees toward the beach. Once they were clear of the trees, Adam kicked his horse in the side and began to go really fast. Eve followed.

"Come on, Daniel, we need to catch up with them," Sarah laughed, kicking her horse in the sides and taking off.

Daniel soon caught up with all of them. The horses galloped down the beach. Everyone's hair blew away from their faces. Soon all of their cheeks were getting red from the wind.

"We should slow down and let the horses rest a little," said Eve.

"You're right," replied Adam. "Let's walk them into the water. They love to go in there."

The four horses whinnied. They sounded happy to get cooled off. Once they got out deep enough in the water, they started to swim.

Sarah slipped off the horse into the water. "Oops! Can someone help me get back on my horse?"

Chapter 6

Eve was next to Sarah, so she reached over and pulled Sarah up onto her horse. Then she reached for Sarah's horse and pulled the two horses together. "Can you slide over onto your horse now?"

"Yes, I can do that. Slipping off just scared me a little, but I'm fine now. Thank you, Eve."

Sarah held on a little tighter this time. They all glided along keeping an eye on the shore. The day was so peaceful. They could hear the birds singing, an elephant making its trumpet noise and the monkeys chattering.

"What's that over there?" Daniel asked. "Something's moving. I hear something that sounds like a bark, but the sound isn't like a dog."

"That is the noise a zebra makes," answered Eve. "They are over there in the clearing beyond those bushes. Would you like to see them up closer?"

"Sure," said Sarah, "I've never seen a zebra up close. At the zoo, they are always way in the back."

"Let's lead the horses to the place where they can get some grass to eat," said Adam. "Here is a good spot."

"Okay, be careful sliding off the horses," said Eve.

"Do we have to be real quiet going over to the zebras?" asked Daniel.

"Yes, that is a good idea. We don't want to scare them," said Eve.

The group tiptoed through the bushes and came out into a beautiful clearing. In a big field, about twelve zebras were eating the grass. Daniel and the others stood and watched them for a while.

Chapter 7

"We can get closer, but be very quiet. We don't want to startle them," said Adam.

Daniel quietly walked over. Holding out his hand, he let the zebra smell him. "He likes me," whispered Daniel. "Can we ride on them too?"

"Yes, but they don't go as fast as horses," replied Eve. "They are shorter too so it's easier to climb up on their backs. Make sure you move slowly so you don't scare them."

Once they were all settled on the backs of zebras, they took a leisurely walk through the pasture. They went to the far side and turned around to come back to the place where they started.

"Okay," said Eve, "we should get out of the sun for a while. There is a beautiful waterfall over through those bushes, and there is a good place to sit and rest. We can pick some strawberries there for a snack."

"That sounds yummy," said Sarah. "I love strawberries. They're my favorite fruit."

Adam led the way. “This is one of my favorite places to come and rest. I also like to talk to God when I come here. He has done so much for us that I take time every day and thank Him for all He has given us.”

“We do that too,” said Daniel. “God doesn’t walk with us like He does with you here. But our parents said we need to pray and thank him. He likes to hear our prayers just like they do.”

“I thank him at night when I say my prayers for all of the fun things that happened during the day,” said Sarah. “And if I get sick, I ask him to make me better. Sometimes I forget to thank him when I am all better. When I remember, I tell him thank you and I am sorry I didn’t thank him sooner.

“Sarah, we should probably start back home,” said Daniel.

“You’re right, we don’t want Mom and Dad to be worried.”

“Thank you for coming to visit us,” said Eve. “It was nice to meet you.”

When they first came to see Adam they had trouble finding “Yahweh’s Express.” This time, they remembered where the time machine was and went right there. They turned and saw Eve talking to a serpent.

“I wish we could warn Eve. God told her she shouldn’t talk to that serpent,” Sarah said sadly.

"I know," replied Daniel, "but I don't think God would want us to do that. Everything would be changed."

"You're right, but it's so beautiful here. Once she eats the apple and shares the fruit with Adam, God will send them out of the garden."

"Yes, but that's what the Bible says happened." replied Daniel.

Daniel and Sarah walked slowly back and climbed in Yahweh's Express. They got back home to the playroom at nine o'clock, the same time as when they left.

"Look, Sarah. Just like last time. We came and left at the same time."

Discussion Questions

Chapter 1

1. What would you use to build a time travel machine?
2. Would you need one of your parents to help you?
3. What do you think about the time not changing at home?
4. Do you think Sarah and Daniel's parents believed they traveled back to the Garden of Eden?

Chapter 2

1. Would your mom be worried about you being close to big animals?
2. Do you and your siblings go to bed at the same time?
3. Do you say bedtime prayers together as a family?
4. After going on a time travel trip do you think you would have trouble sleeping?

Chapter 3

1. What do you think it would be like to be able to talk with Adam and Eve?
2. Do you like to play in the water?
3. Have you ever gone swimming with dolphins? Did you get to ride on its back?
4. Have you been close to sea turtles? What was it like?

Chapter 4

1. Do you have gold fish or tropical fish? Who takes care of them?
2. Are you usually hungry after swimming?
3. Do you have a vegetable garden? What do you grow?

4. Do you help at home to fix meals?

Chapter 5

1. Have you ever been horseback riding? Do you ride bareback or with a saddle?
2. What do you think about holding on to the horse's mane?
3. Would you like to ride on a horse that was running?
4. How do you think you would feel if you slipped off a horse and fell in the water?

Chapter 6

1. Would it make you feel better to ride with someone after falling into the water?
2. What noise did the zebra make? Where have you seen one?
3. How would you feel being so close to the zebra's?

Chapter 7

1. What do you think it would be like to ride on a zebra?
2. Have you ever seen a waterfall? Where was it?
3. Do you have a place where you feel real close to God? Tell me about it.
4. What would you do if you saw Eve talking to the serpent?

33502275R00020

Made in the USA
San Bernardino, CA
04 May 2016